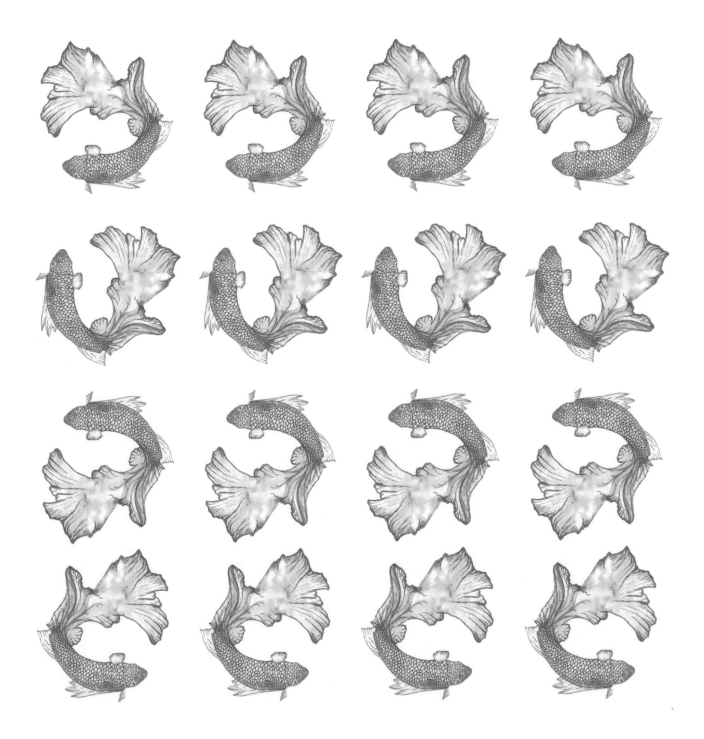

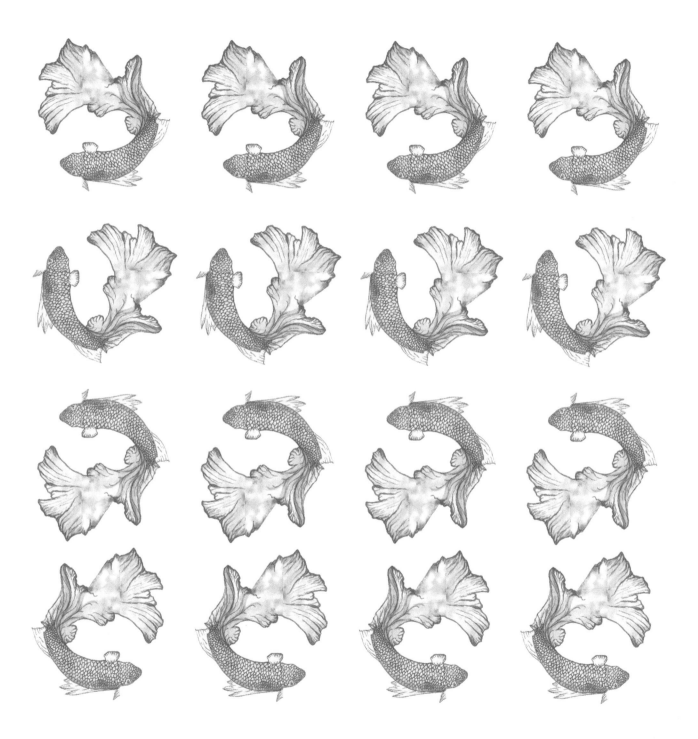

Mr McGimpsey's Kites

Written by
A P Pullan

Illustrated by
Karen Shakespeare

ISBN: 9781082008399

A P Pullan is a teacher based in South Ayrshire. He has written two children's novels, *The Crying Wind* and *A Polar Bear Called Forth*. He enjoys sailing and eating scones.

Karen Shakespeare is an art tutor based in North Ayrshire. When not making wonderful ceramic art, she loves eating cakes.

On the beach he'd peg them

under the deep blue sky.

People gasped at his creations,

sailing up, so very high.

In winter, he'd fly a snowman

topped with a golden hat,

with snowflakes falling all around him.

Well, how did he do that?

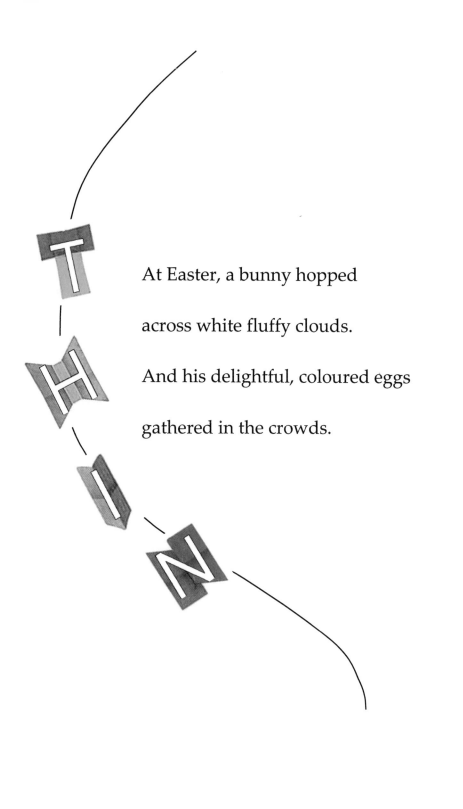

At Easter, a bunny hopped

across white fluffy clouds.

And his delightful, coloured eggs

gathered in the crowds.

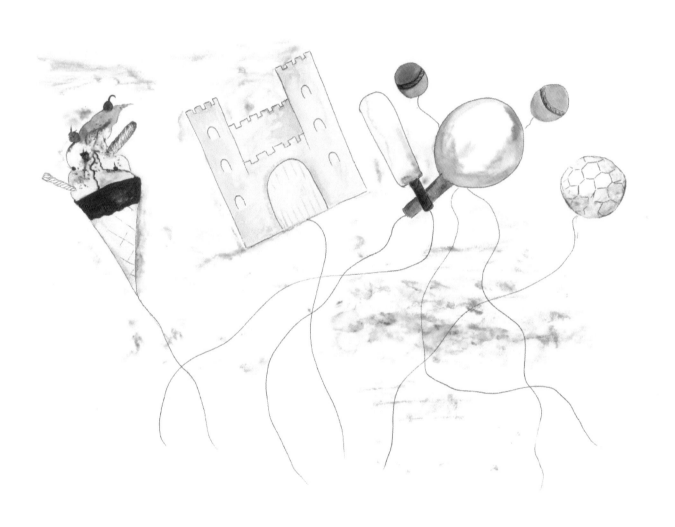

In summer he'd fly huge ice creams

all topped with fruit and sweets.

Sandcastles, bats and balls!

What a sight! What a treat!

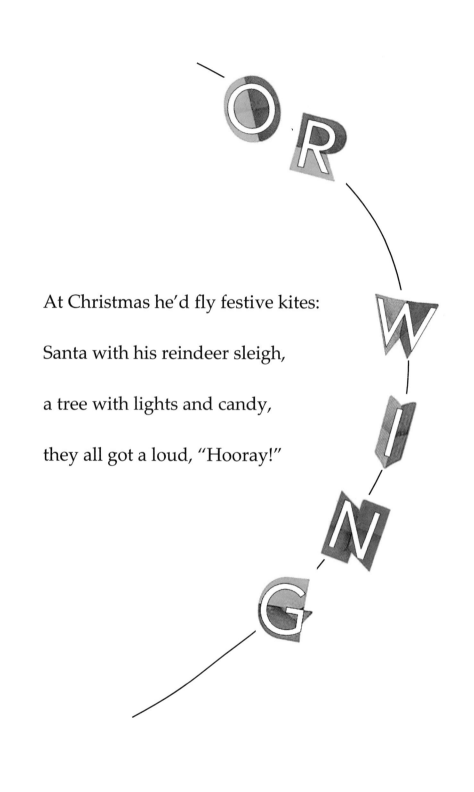

At Christmas he'd fly festive kites:

Santa with his reindeer sleigh,

a tree with lights and candy,

they all got a loud, "Hooray!"

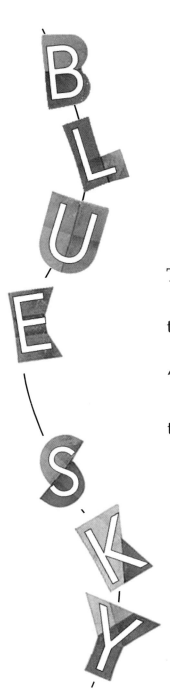

BLUE SKY

The day eight kites were flying

the Mayor gave McGimpsey a call,

"One last kite is all we're asking

to say goodbye, that's all?"

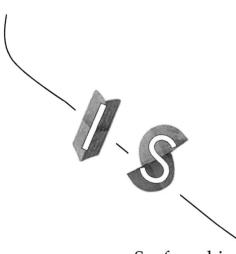

So, from his tree-top workshop,

through the night till first sun

saw, knock, drill, bang!

At last, his work was done.

The town awoke that morning,

to a flock of exotic birds

who flew among beautiful fish.

Well, everyone was lost for words.

But Mr McGimpsey had vanished

without thanks for what he'd made.

As the months and years wore on

his kites would tear and fade.

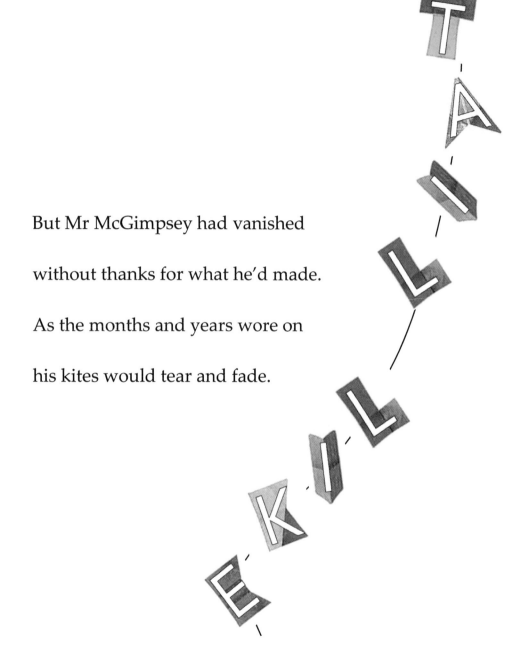

Then a lady had an idea,

and rang the mayor that night.

"I've just had a baby girl so,

I'll celebrate with a kite!"

With her baby's name upon it,

flew a dove all pink and white.

Soon a beautiful display of all kinds

turned the sky again so bright.

From far and wide, people came

to see the spectacular sights.

The town with the colourful sky,

all thanks to McGimpsey's kites.

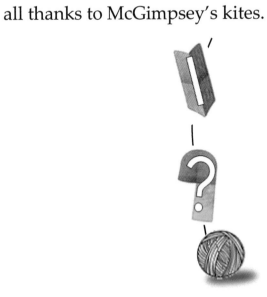

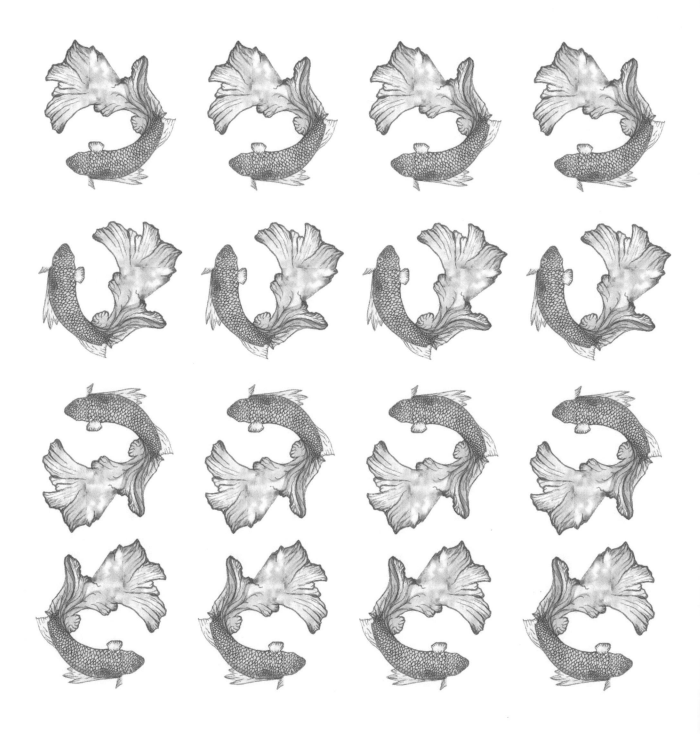

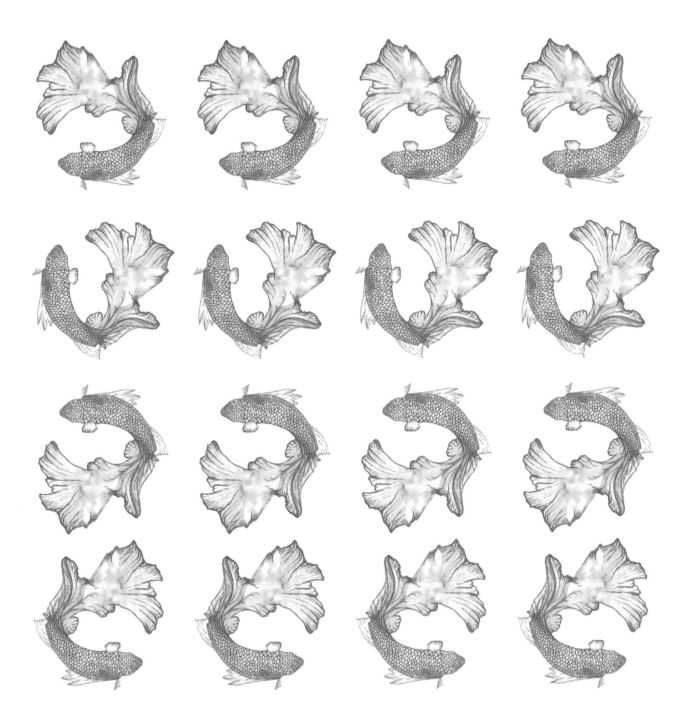

Printed in Great Britain
by Amazon